THE LOST BOYS OF
NATINGA

A SCHOOL FOR SUDAN'S YOUNG REFUGEES

JUDY WALGREN

HOUGHTON MIFFLIN COMPANY
BOSTON 1998

In loving memory of Fred Cuny, who shared my passion for Africa

Acknowledgments

This book would not have been possible without the support of many people. My deepest *asante sanas* to Julia Dean, director of JD&A; *Dallas Morning News* assistant managing editor, John Davidson, photo editor, Robert Hart, and office manager, Karen Griffen; Mirella Riccardi, photographer and writer; Shermakaye Bass; and Carolyn Roumeguere, my soul sister in Kenya.

Special thanks to Norwegian People's Aid, especially to Helge Rohn, David Evans, Sorcha Fennel, Dan Eiffe, and Peter Dut, for supporting me on my many trips to Kenya and the Sudan; to Philip Thon, from the FACE Foundation; to Friends in the West; and to Juma, the greatest convoy leader working in southern Sudan.

I would like to extend my gratitude to Norma Jean Sawicki, who gave me the chance to pursue this dream, and to Judy Levin, who walked me through this book with her undivided attention and patience, and to Amy Flynn, who found it and got it done.

My greatest appreciation goes to the children of Natinga, who showered me with so much love as I explored their lives. I pray that one day the civil war will end so that they can experience peace and all of its blessings.

Finally, I could not have survived the grueling six months in the Horn of Africa without the support and encouragement of my father, mother, sister, and brother. I am forever beholden to you all.

The text of this book is set in 12.5 point Joanna.

Library of Congress Cataloging-in-Publication Data

Walgren, Judy.
   The lost boys of Natinga: a school for Sudan's young refugees / Judy Walgren.
      p.   cm.
   Summary: Describes daily life at Natinga, a refugee camp and school established in 1993 in southern Sudan for boys forced from their homes by that country's civil war.
   ISBN 0-395-70558-4
   1. Ethiopians—Refugee children—Sudan—Pictorial works—Juvenile literature. 2. Sudanese—Ethiopia—Pictorial works—Juvenile literature. [1. Sudan—History. 2. Refugees.]   I. Title.
   HQ792.E75W35   1998
   305.23'08691—dc21   97-32210
                                                     CIP AC

Printed in Singapore
TWP 10 9 8 7 6 5 4 3 2 1

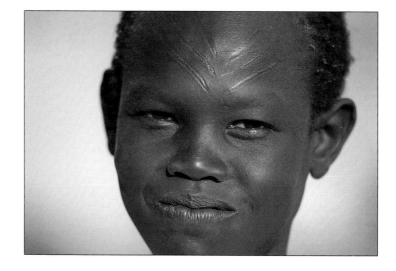

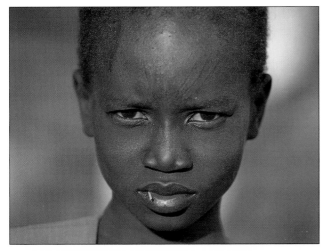

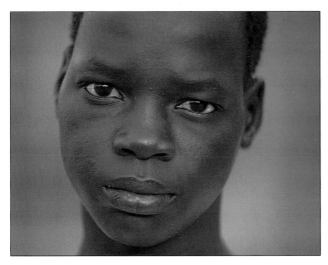

CONTENTS

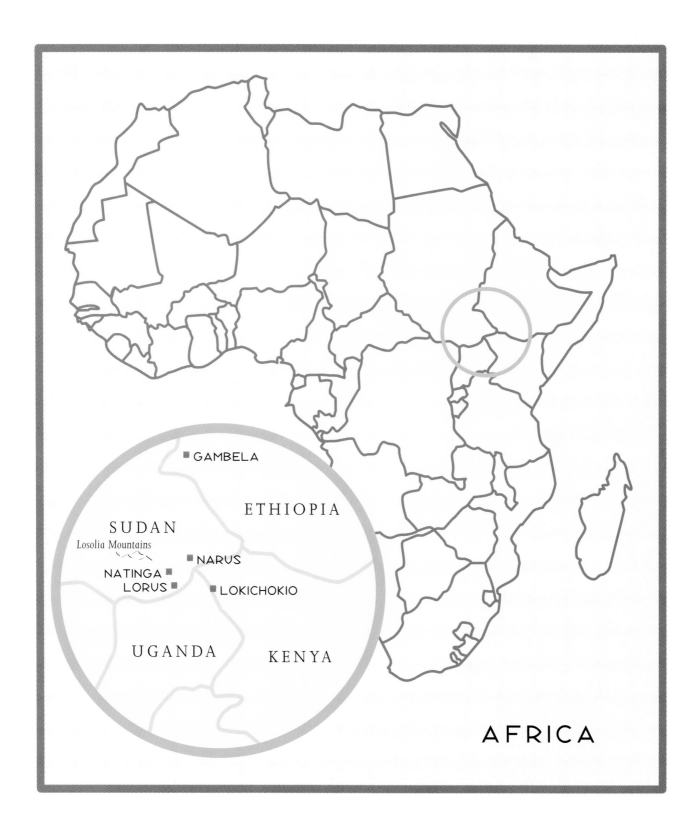

GAMBELA

ETHIOPIA

SUDAN

Losolia Mountains

NARUS

NATINGA
LORUS

LOKICHOKIO

UGANDA

KENYA

AFRICA

I am a photographer for the *Dallas Morning News*. I first visited Africa in 1989 when my boss, John Davidson, sent a writer and me to do a story about the civil war in Sudan. We stayed for a month and a half, cruising the bush with the southern rebels, walking through crowds of refugees, and counting the number of seconds it took for the shells to fall.

Between 1992 and 1993 I was sent to Africa twice, to cover different news stories in different parts of the continent. Each time I wondered how the people in southern Sudan were getting on. I heard that the rebels were losing ground and that there was no end in sight to the fighting. I had seen the war being fought, yet there were few reports about it in American newspapers.

After I flew back to Nairobi, Kenya, I began hearing stories about large groups of boys living in schools in displaced persons camps in southern Sudan. Some people said the rebels were using these schools to train the boys to fight in the southern army. Others could not explain why the groups emerged. I wanted to talk with the boys.

1

Natinga is one of these schools. When I first arrived, hundreds of small boys wearing rags came running to meet my car. "Do you have one pen?" they begged. "One piece of paper for me?" I was surprised by their requests, expecting to be asked for money or candy.

During that first visit I could stay only a little more than a day, photographing the boys at school, doing daily chores, dancing, and preparing meals. When I left, I had enough information for a newspaper story about young boys who had been forced to leave their families because of the civil war. Many of their parents had been killed. A few of the boys told me that the rebel army had forced them to walk to Ethiopia, but very few regretted leaving their homes. They believed they would be dead if they had stayed in their villages.

When I returned to Dallas, I wanted to stop strangers on the street to show them the photos of the boys in Natinga and to talk about their lives. Every day those boys struggle to get food, to stay healthy, and to go to school. My house and car and the supermarkets where I shop are luxuries they can barely imagine.

To write this book, I went back to Natinga. For almost two months I lived in a hut that had once housed some chickens. After two bouts with malaria, an infestation of chicken mites (small insects that live on chickens and loved the down lining of my sleeping bag), a leg ulcer from an infected mosquito bite, and three days without food, I was ready to go home. But I still think about those children and their teachers, who cannot leave. They have no other home.

I pray that the war will end and that they will be able to rejoin their families. Their lives have been changed forever, but they are trying hard to prepare themselves for a future in which they will be responsible adults, governing their own country.

The civil war in Sudan began in 1983, when the South rebelled against the North and demanded its own government. Since then, more than one and a half million people have died.

David Majok, a commander in the southern army, says that all of Sudan's laws come from Khartoum, the capital in the North. Since Sudan gained its independence from the British in 1956, the northerners have made Islam the law of the land. Most of them are Arabs, and they prevent the Christians and the animists (people who follow traditional tribal religions) from entering the government and even from following their own traditions. Commander Majok says, "In the North, anywhere you go, they call a southerner an *abeed*, or slave. There is still a lot of slavery in the North, mainly using children from the South."

There are also economic reasons for the war. All of Sudan's natural resources—gold, oil, and fertile land for farming—are located in the

These rebel soldiers are waiting for orders. Some of them are as young as fourteen.

3

South, but the cities and industries are in the North. If the country is divided, the government and people of the North would not be able to profit from the South's resources.

The southern army calls itself the Sudanese People's Liberation Army, or SPLA. Most of its members are Dinka, which is the largest tribe in the South. For the first eight years of the war, the army occupied the countryside and most southern Sudanese towns. Then, in August of 1991, three high-ranking officers from the Nuer tribe broke away from SPLA. They felt the Dinka were not supporting members of the army from the other tribes in the South. After the southern forces divided, northern government troops were able to capture most of the southern towns.

Both the northern and southern armies have used the "scorched earth" policy. When they attack, they burn villages and crops and steal cattle and food. This destruction forces people to depend on the soldiers and allows the army to take control, but the policy has created millions of refugees.

Since the war began, tens of thousands of children and adolescents have been separated from their families or orphaned. These young people are living in displaced persons camps in Sudan or refugee camps in Kenya and Ethiopia. Natinga is named for a small village at the base of the foothills of the Losolia Mountains. It is the home of about 2,000 boys from many different tribes and for hundreds of families who come and go, seeking food, clothing, shelter, and safety.

The camp at Natinga was created in 1993 after a truck of rebel soldiers overturned near the village of Lorus. The soldiers unloaded the food from the demolished truck and set up camp. The leader of the rebel movement, Dr. John Garang, was told there was a reliable water supply, so he decided to set up a base in Lorus.

At the same time, the rebels decided that some of the boys should be moved to Natinga from less secure areas. The new camp could be well hidden in the mountains, and the soldiers in Lorus could protect it. Soon rebel soldiers began moving children to Natinga from all over southern Sudan.

In the beginning of the war, Sudanese adults and children sought safety in Ethiopia. In 1987, rebel soldiers rounded up many of the southern boys and took them to refugee camps and schools. They did not take the girls because many of the tribes do not believe that girls need to be educated. Also, the women and girls were in less danger because Sudanese women do not fight in the rebel armies. The southern soldiers and their commanders now argue that the boys would have been killed or taken as slaves by the Khartoum forces if they had stayed in their villages. They say they want to keep the boys safe and to educate them so there will be young men ready to govern southern Sudan when it is free.

Many organizations, including UNICEF, do not believe the soldiers. They say the rebels are preparing the boys to fight in the army. Other people say the rebels keep the boys in camps so that their troops can eat the food that relief organizations donate to the children.

There is probably some truth to both statements. Workers at Kakuma Refugee Camp in Kenya say the rebels do come and take boys

Since the war began, the boys have walked thousands of miles through southern Sudan, Kenya, and Ethiopia. Often they traveled at night so the government troops could not see them.

to fight, but they also say that the boys want to go with the soldiers. Their families and friends have been killed, and until the war is over there is no place for them to go. They can stay in refugee camps and try to prepare for peace and self-government or they can fight.

Peter Maket, a student in Natinga, says, "We remember our lives before and what stopped that life: the war. When I was ten years old, I was keeping the cattle in my father's house. It was good and I had balance in my life."

Peter was part of the earliest group of children and teenagers who walked to Ethiopia. Many died before they could reach the refugee camp. Some were killed by hostile tribes or by northern soldiers. Some died of starvation, animal attacks, or disease. Others drowned while crossing streams and rivers or ate poisonous plants when their food ran out.

Once the children, families, and teachers arrived in Natinga, they built houses similar to the ones they lived in before the war. The tukels are made from long grasses cut in the mountains, which they tie to wooden posts. Mud carried up from the stream covers the outside of the huts.

In the late 1980s, there were about 66,000 boys between the ages of six and eighteen among the 300,000 refugees in the Itung camp in Ethiopia. Then, in 1990, the Ethiopian leader was overthrown. The new leader gave the Sudanese army permission to invade the refugee camps, so they were no longer safe.

Before the Khartoum troops arrived from the North, the boys returned to southern Sudan. The SPLA split the children into groups, taking them to different areas. Civilians were being attacked by government troops, and members of SPLA say that keeping the boys together would have been too dangerous.

Sixteen-year-old Stephen Abol has been on the run since he was seven. His group of boys went to Kapoeta in southern Sudan from Ethiopia. They had walked for a month.

"At this time, I was very thin," Stephen remembers. "We were walking during the rainy season and we had no plastic sheeting. Many people died along the way, including my three friends. I thought I might die." The boys were also attacked by government soldiers.

Once inside Kapoeta, the boys constructed grass huts, called tukels in the Dinka language, and the teachers began classes. But in 1992 government soldiers captured Kapoeta from the rebels, and the boys again had to escape. This time they walked to eastern Equatoria and joined the boys living in Moli. That journey took nine days. Then, in February of 1993, when the government attacked a rebel base near Moli, the boys packed their knapsacks and walked to Natinga, another month-long journey.

"I do not know what will happen tomorrow. I only know that today I am in Natinga," Stephen says. "It is God who knows what will happen in the future. My condition is difficult, but I just hand myself to God and ask him to take me in his hands."

Kuol Atem Bol, the administrator of the Natinga school, has lived with the boys since they arrived in Ethiopia in 1987. He was the director of a primary school until November 1983, when he fled to Ethiopia with his family to escape the fighting. He hopes that they will all be able to stay in Natinga until the war ends. Everyone is tired of setting up homes and schools, then having to flee when the government planes find them and begin bombing.

As the sun rises, the sound of a hammer striking a rusted wheel rim can be heard throughout the camp. The boys in their tukels wake up. Three to four boys sleep on grass mats in each of the small huts, which are built in groups called compounds. Usually a few older boys live in each compound so they can help the younger children cook and clean. The adults live in their own compounds if they have their families with them, in single huts if they are alone.

After one of the older boys sounds the wake-up call, everyone gets out of bed and wanders down to the river to bathe. Then the children dress in their school uniforms and walk to school. The uniforms, though tattered and pieced together from donated clothing, add a sense of order to their lives. The boys take good care of their white T-shirts and shorts, washing them in the river as often as they can.

A few boys stop at the hut of Pious Kara Quitino, a teacher, to use

SCHOOL

A formal class.

9

his hairbrush, one of the few in the camp. Pious checks the children's hair for lice. If he finds them, he shaves the child's head with a rusted straight-edge razor and scrubs the bare scalp with water.

The people in southern Sudan value education very highly. Education has always been denied them, and they believe they cannot be free or equal without it. When the British controlled Sudan, they built most of the schools in the North. Southerners have always resented their having to travel to Khartoum for higher education. When the British left, they gave southern Sudan to the North, but an educational system was never developed. The southerners believe that the government does not want to educate them because without education they will be easier to control. Also, they do not want to go to the Muslim religious schools because they are not Muslim. The southerners believe that having their own schools is the answer to making their lives better and to preparing for life after the war.

There are two types of classes, formal and informal. The six formal classes are sponsored by Friends in the West, an American relief organization. The grade levels are the same as those in the United States, and the students study from American books. The children in these classes were chosen because they had the highest scores on exams given in the

The children in the formal classes have white uniforms made from material sent by the relief agency. Those without uniforms put outfits together from the clothing donated to the camp.

Most informal classes are taught down by the riverbed.

informal classes. Many have never been to school, and even some of the older ones must start in first grade.

Formal classes are held in the two open-air churches in Natinga. Before school begins, the students break branches from trees and sweep the dirt floors in and around the school. They wipe the dust off the log pews and hang their handmade bookbags on the ends of the posts. Then they hurry down to the river to again wash their hands, arms, and legs before classes begin.

During roll call, the students stand in rows. The first-grade teachers, Consetta Ayuak and Abraham Chol, walk up and down the aisles inspecting them. The teachers constantly stress the importance of keeping their bodies, clothing, and living areas clean.

There are few books available, so the formal classes must be small. Most of the children and young adults and even some of the older men attend informal classes, held under the trees next to the riverbed. There the students sit on rocks or empty cooking-oil cans around a chalkboard propped against a tree. The teachers use tattered maps, old math books, and materials copied from textbooks.

Pious Kara Quitino shows one of his students how to make the number 8.

Consetta Ayuak gathers her students' workbooks when class is finished. There are not enough books, so some must copy the textbooks by hand into blank notebooks.

Classes are taught in English. The teachers believe that the children must learn to communicate with people from the West, mainly the United States. Many of the boys already know English because the British ruled Sudan for many years. Dinka is the second most common language. Arabic is the third, learned by children who attended the few Koranic (Islamic) schools in the South. Some of the children from the bush areas speak only their tribal language, but they are eager to learn the language that the Americans speak. Learning a common language is important in a country in which each of forty-seven tribes speaks a different language.

Sharon Hales and Fred Magumba, workers for Friends in the West, go to Natinga whenever possible to check on the progress of the students. Sharon believes formal classes are better for the children because the classroom setting adds some structure to their lives. They have less time to think about the past.

During an arithmetic lesson in a formal first-grade class, Pious notices that one of his students is struggling to write the numbers. He takes a twig from a broom and scratches the numbers from 1 to 10 in

the dirt floor. Then he places the twig in the boy's hand and helps him write the figures. At first the boy struggles, but after four tries, his 3s and 8s look much better than before.

Pious says it's difficult to teach when there are not enough books, blackboards, chalk, pens, pencils, and paper. He says, "We have great difficulties because we are running the schools outside under the trees. When it is raining, we have no choice but to send the children back to their tukels. We cannot even get a roll of plastic sheeting to make a roof over our heads. The place where we cut grass for the roofs and buildings is very far away, and if we have to send the children there to collect the grass, it will take them away from their schoolwork."

In another formal first grade, students read aloud from an American textbook. "The doll is a rag doll. The doll has on a bib. The doll has on a hat. The hat is red." The teacher, Consetta Ayuak, says, "At first, when we introduced the new teaching material from Friends in the West, the children were shy about trying to learn it. They did not seem to like it.

But when they realized that the books were not going to disappear, that they were theirs to use to learn, they began to like the material."

The classes have made the children more assertive and confident. They no longer run away when a stranger greets them. Instead, they shout, "How are you?" and "I am fine!" to visitors. Some of the children do not understand what they are saying. They are simply repeating what they have heard their teachers say.

There are only four girls in Consetta's class. They are from families that moved to Natinga for food and security. Often, when Consetta asks for volunteers to read out loud, only the boys respond. Consetta asks, "What about the girls? I am not only teaching the boys!"

In Sudan, the women are not as well educated as the men, a cultural tradition that some Natinga teachers hope to change. Consetta says, "The Mahdi or my tribe, the Ochole, both from eastern Equatoria, have always educated the girls along with the boys. The Dinka are beginning to see that it is good to have their daughters educated so they won't remain in the kitchen." She is the only woman among the twenty-five teachers in Natinga.

After the English and arithmetic lessons, the students study world geography. They can all point out Sudan on an old map of Africa. They also study history from old Kenyan schoolbooks. But without classrooms or enough books, their education covers only the basics: reading, writing, and arithmetic. Both the students and their teachers agree it is better than nothing at all.

The classes finish at one o'clock and the children and teachers sing "Long Live Natinga School." Everyone gathers for the closing prayer, led by Abraham. Sitting on the front pew is Gabriel Deng, a thin boy dressed in tattered clothes. Gaping wounds run up and down his legs. Gabriel says his prayer in the Dinka language. In English his prayer says, "Father, you will deliver our souls and you will direct our lives. Father, do not kill your children. Please deliver your young generation from this suffering. Father, please deliver us from the war situation we are living in."

Gabriel tells me: "When the war is finished, life will be good. When the war stops, the children will be able to learn in a proper place, in a real school, with books and classrooms."

FOOD

The cooking hut has no sides so that smoke can escape. The children stir a mixture of flour and water until it is firm enough to be scooped up with their hands.

Every year during the rainy season, violent thunderstorms turn the road to Natinga to mud. Trucks get stuck, and it can take a month for the drivers to dig the vehicles out. Usually the food trucks carry maize, which is a kind of corn, and sorghum, a plant whose grain can be boiled and eaten, ground into flour for bread, or cooked with water to make porridge.

After an unusually heavy month of rain and infrequent food shipments, the last of the food brought by the World Food Programme, a relief organization, has been eaten. Emergency food, saved from deliveries earlier in the year, is also gone. The children begin to search the forest for grass and leaves to eat. They have been without food before and have learned over the years which plants are edible and which are poisonous.

Food is a constant problem for the camp. At first Natinga received food from Norwegian People's Aid. For a year it supplied Natinga with a well-rounded diet, sending dried fish, rabbits, and salt with the sacks of grain. Then the World Food Programme asked to take over the food delivery to Natinga. Since it is a large and powerful organization, the smaller Norwegian group agreed.

Unfortunately, the World Food Programme workers estimated that there were 2,500 people living in the Natinga area—only half the Norwegians' estimate. It is difficult to determine the exact population of the camp because it is always changing. Boys leave in search of better food and schools. Others arrive. In any event, the seventy-six tons of food that Norwegian People's Aid had sent each month was cut to thirty-eight tons.

Every Tuesday, food for the week is distributed by the teachers or older boys to the children responsible for cooking the meals that week.

When they run low on food, the children search the forest for grass and leaves to eat.

Normally, one hundred and twelve bags are distributed for the entire camp. This morning, there are only fifteen bags of sorghum. That is not enough for the entire camp, so the director of the school decides to give out the seventy bags of grain that were being saved for planting.

In 1993, Natinga had fifty days without food. "The army in the area supported us as much as they could with food. The boys collected leaves from trees that looked similar to those in their home area. But some chose the wrong leaves," says Kuol Atem Bol. Thirteen children died.

The boys line up behind Deng Arok, the teacher in charge of food distribution, and wait patiently. An older boy uses a tin coffee cup to measure each ration. He carefully pours the grain into empty food bags, and the boys take the loads away on top of their heads.

After the grain is distributed, the children prepare the food for cooking. It takes many hours to pound the grain into flour and to sift out the grain shells from the flour.

Fourteen-year-old James Manut Chol works

under the shade of a tree. Trickles of sweat run slowly down his forehead, which is lined with the traditional Dinka scars. He puts the sorghum in a hollow log standing on one end, then uses a huge pole to mash it.

When James finishes grinding the grain into flour, he pours it into a large wooden bowl and takes it to the kitchen, a grass hut without walls. Three pots of water sit on fires in the hut and smoke billows out of the roof through a small hole in the top. As boys light each fire with hot coals, they chant in Dinka: "Dit mac ku kor akon," which means, "The fire is big and the elephant is small." It is a traditional good luck chant for fire lighting.

As the water begins to boil, the boys add the yellow flour to the pots, stirring the gruel with a branch as it begins to thicken. When the mixture turns into a gooey porridge, it is ready to eat.

During the morning school break, the children go back to their tukels to collect their battered tin bowls and to see if the food is ready. Usually there is a little food, so four or five boys will share a small bowl of porridge. If there is no food, the boys will play ball or look over their schoolwork until class begins again.

Boys lined up for the weekly food distribution.

The grain must be ground into flour by hand. Then stones and the inedible parts of the grain are sifted out of the flour using a box with fishnet on the bottom.

A typical meal for children in a camp for displaced people is a cup of porridge for each child twice a day. Because there is a shortage of food, however, the children get only a half cup twice a day. As soon as the mixture hits the bowl, the boys use their hands to scoop it into their mouths. They do not lift their heads from the bowl until it is clean.

When they are finished eating, the children gather up their schoolbooks and return to class. There will be no more food until evening.

The children are used to being hungry. "If there is food, we eat between nine and ten-thirty in the morning," says twelve-year-old Michael Kur James. "Then we must wait until five in the afternoon or

Many children share this bowl of boiled sorghum.

The children unload sacks of grain from the stalled Norwegian People's Aid truck.

later for the second cup of food. I try and sleep in the afternoon to stop the hunger pains in my stomach. It is the only way I can stand it."

Three days pass and food has still not arrived. Kuol, the teachers, and the children begin to panic. A meeting of the teachers and the heads of the families living in the camp is called to make a plan. They send an emergency message to Norwegian People's Aid, asking them to ship a few bags of grain.

Soon Ajok Atem, a southern Sudanese man working with the Norwegian group, arrives in Lorus with thirty-eight trucks. He is not going to Natinga but to Chukadum, a large village farther up the road. An SPLA commander tells him about Natinga's food shortage and, after visiting the empty storage areas, Ajok decides to take the food from a broken truck and give it to Natinga. He says he cannot let the children go hungry while food just sits on the ground. Fifty children walk down the hill, place the heavy bags on top of their heads, and, smiling, carry the food back up the mountain. The eleven tons of corn will last ten days.

The teachers also show the students how to grow their own food. Caring for crops will take them away from their studies, but the teachers hope that if the children can produce some of their own food, they will not be so frightened when the bags of sorghum and corn are late. After the first heavy rains of the year arrive in April, the children rise at six in the morning and walk to the five fields by the Natinga River. A few days each week, the teachers work alongside their students, showing them how to clear the land and prepare it for planting.

"This is the normal life of children in southern Sudan," says Beda Machar Deng. "When children are eight years old, they assist their

A three-year-old boy uses a panga to clear the land so he can plant okra seeds.

mothers with cultivating their plot of land in the village. When the sons are ten, they have to cultivate their own food while the daughters help their mothers in the fields. All of these children come from a pastoral culture, keeping cattle and growing food, and if they miss these lessons, they will have a very hard time going back to their cultures after the war is finished."

Unfortunately, most of the children in the camp do not have families to share the work, so they have less time to study. Yet many of their home villages did not have schools at all, so they learned only how to take care of cattle and goats and to grow crops.

The students turn the sandy soil with handmade hoes and pangas—large knives used for cutting grass and chopping down trees. The small children use sticks or their hands to pull up weeds.

After the ground is prepared, they must wait for one rain before planting the seedlings. There must be about thirty rains in

The land must be cultivated using simple tools.

the following three months for the seeds to sprout and grow into mature plants. Irrigating the fields is impossible, so the success of the crops depends completely on the weather. If the rains are plentiful, the children will be able to harvest in three months. There have been several thunderstorms already, but the teachers still worry that the weather will again be too dry, as it was the year before.

"If the camp can produce its own seeds from a successful crop, agencies will be able to use the money that they spend on seeds for Natinga for other items such as salt, medicines, and oil," Beda Machar Deng explains.

One day during the planting, Chol Jok Kuir sits on a log by the edge of the field and wipes the sweat from his face. He came to Natinga with his mother in 1991, after his father was killed by militia forces. As he describes his father's death and the nine-day walk without food from one refugee camp to another, tears stream down his face. "I do not ever want to be hungry again," he says.

The medical clinic in Natinga is a large tukel. Fifteen beds line the walls of the dirt-floored hut. Sick children lie sweating in the beds. They are suffering from scarlet fever, diarrhea, hepatitis, mumps, or malaria.

Stephen Abol is one of three medical assistants in the camp. His days are long, and his work is made difficult by the lack of supplies. He needs antibiotics for infections, chloroquine for malaria, injections for typhoid and meningitis, medicine to kill intestinal worms, and bandages for wounds.

Stephen's father was killed by the government soldiers in 1984 while trying to keep them from taking his children to use as slaves in the North. In 1985, when Stephen was seven, the SPLA went to his village to round up the boys. Stephen left his family and walked to an Ethiopian refugee camp with a group of boys and rebel soldiers. From

Outside the clinic, a boy waits for a medical assistant. He suffers from intestinal worms, but there is no medicine in the camp to help him.

27

age eleven to fourteen, he lived in this camp on the Ethiopian border and was trained by a Sudanese physician.

He says, "There is no porridge in the morning. There are no biscuits for the children. The diet here is terrible. The people are malnourished, which makes them more susceptible to disease. They sleep in dirty clothes with dirty bedding because there is no soap to wash their things. Sick children cannot roam the area searching for food, fresh leaves, and vegetables to supplement their diet, so they lie in their beds and waste away."

The camp is so low on medical supplies that Stephen sends an emergency message to Kenya, but heavy rains have washed out the road and the trucks cannot come. Finally, Sharon and Fred from Friends in the West plan an airdrop of the most necessary supplies.

On the day of the airdrop, the women and younger children leave the camp at 3:30 in the morning, for airdrops can be dangerous. Many boys remember an airdrop in Pochala when the cargo landed on top of a tukel, killing one person and breaking the backs of two cows. The older boys and the teachers stay behind to watch for the plane and collect the cargo. Soldiers from Lorus perch on the hilltops around the camp so they can watch where the cargo falls if the pilot misses the soccer field, the planned target. Everyone waits for the sound of the plane with great excitement.

At 5:30, the rebels take their radio up to Natinga so Kuol can communicate with the people in the plane. They climb the hill on the other side of the soccer field and wait under a large Gumeal tree for a message from the pilot.

On another hill, ten boys build a huge fire, putting green leaves on the flames to create smoke. The pilot will look for this signal before dropping the supplies. Another fire is made directly on the field, and a large piece of white plastic sheeting is held down with rocks. This is the pilot's target.

The first plane leaves Lokichockio at 6 a.m. and flies to Thiet, a village north of Natinga. A second plane flies over the mountains on its way to Nasir. Again and again planes appear overhead, but the one designated for Natinga does not arrive. By 10:30, the radio man, Kuol, and Beda give up and return to their compounds.

The next day Sharon sends Kuol a message: medical supplies will be
dropped at 10 a.m. This time the camp is not evacuated to Lorus. The
soldiers do not come and scout the area from the mountains. The children stay in school. After the first disappointment, the teachers do not
believe that the plane will actually arrive.

At 10:30, the plane makes its first pass over the field. The older
boys run from school to set the signal fires and lay the plastic sheeting
in place. As the plane passes the field a second time, its door opens,
and two plastic trash bags fall out of the sky. The packages hit an area
above the field next to the tukels, but fortunately they do not fall on
the huts.

The children eagerly tear open the bags but find only syringes, a
few malaria pills, some antibiotic injections, and a box of aspirin.
Many of the supplies they were expecting, such as bandages, rehydra-
tion salts, and medicine to kill parasites were not sent. Stephen shakes

*The fire helps the pilot see the
target for the airdrop.*

29

Inside the clinic, sick children wait to get well. Without medicine their illnesses can last a long time.

his head. The camp is not prepared for the outbreaks of malaria and scarlet fever that he knows will come.

Twelve-year-old James Riak has been in the clinic for a month. He has jaundice caused by hepatitis, and Stephen says he will be sick for another six months without proper medical treatment. "I feel my whole body failing me," James says, "I feel so very bad I do not know what to do. At night, I hurt. During the day, I hurt. There are never any changes." The antibiotics dropped from the plane will not be enough to cure him.

Twenty-three-year-old David Dau Lulak has an alternative to waiting for the medical supplies: "When we do not have commercial medicine, I can make medicine from the roots of the trees. When there is no medicine, you can use your mind and find one of the elders who can show you which tree to use.

"There are some animals whose meat can make a treatment, such as the hyena. When someone has swollen lymph glands, the hyena's fat will reduce the swelling and you can put it into a wound and fight infection. Malaria can be treated with the Pach tree bark. You can chew it, and it can relieve the symptoms. Sometimes when there is no tree, you can use the bladder and liver from the goats to help malaria symptoms. When we were in Bor we had many traditional doctors. But that was before the war. Now, many of the people are dead, and soon there will be no one left to teach us the old ways."

The traditional medical treatments do not work as well as modern antibiotics, but they do help. Often they make the patient more comfortable while the body heals itself.

The living conditions in Natinga contribute to its health problems. Between two and four thousand people are crowded together. Before the war, families lived in large compounds in the villages surrounded by gardens and fields of sorghum and corn. Natinga must stay small so that the government's bombers cannot see it from the air.

The camp is littered with sun-bleached fish bones, parts of dead goats, chicken feet, carcasses of dead rabbits, dirty bandages, weeds, and garbage. There are no pits for burning trash, so people throw their garbage outside their compounds.

Every two months, the teachers organize a general cleaning of the camp. The children use hoes and pangas to chop down the tall weeds growing around the tukels. They use leafy branches to sweep the garbage away from the dwelling areas. This helps keep away the snakes, mosquitoes, and insects during the rains. After they put the trash in piles, they use empty food sacks and their heads to carry it to the "dump," just outside the camp area.

Finding clean water is also a problem. There are no springs or perma-

Clean-up in Natinga.

Water is collected in the riverbed by digging holes in the sand and waiting for them to fill.

nent rivers near the camp. The UNICEF water team has tried to find water four times. The workers dug deep holes in the ground with a drilling rig, but they did not find a water source large enough to supply the entire camp. Only one bore hole was successful, and the pump broke from overuse after a week.

During the dry season, the boys walk to Lorus, a thirty-minute hike. They collect water from the bore holes there in battered plastic containers and walk back to Natinga with the receptacles balanced on their heads. The water in Lorus is salty and tastes bad, so occasionally the students hike an hour and a half into the Losolia mountains to collect sweet water from the springs.

The children dig deep holes in the dry riverbed until a trickle of water seeps into the bottom of the hole. These "wells" are usually more than ten feet deep. The children spend hours scooping the water from the hole.

Badrodin Kamal remembers a time in 1993 when they went for months without rain. "Our first dry season, we waited for a small pool of water to form in the rocks. We collected one small bucket of water for bathing and washing clothes. The boys would wash their blankets and clothes in the water until it was black. Then we would pour the water in the sand and dig a small hole a few feet away. The water would be filtered and come up into the hole clean," he explained.

"At first there were ten of us doing this, then more children came and repeated the process. You would wash yourselves on the rocks, collect the water in a bucket, and dig the hole in the sand again and again," he said. "It was really terrible, I tell you."

In fact, although filtering the water through sand makes it look clean, it is not. Germs survive the filtering process and cause many illnesses.

During the rainy season, the dry riverbed turns into a swiftly running river. The brown water roars over the marble boulders and winds down through the camp.

Rain is therefore a mixed blessing for Natinga. A serious downpour will bring enough water for a few days and help the new crops to survive for another ten days. But rain turns the roads from Kenya into mud and stops shipments of food and medicine.

There is usually an outbreak of diarrhea following each heavy rain. The ground is hard and rocky, so there is no way to make a hole large enough for a permanent toilet. The camp's two toilets are made from piles of mud with a hole dug in the middle. After two to three months, they will be covered with dirt and new toilets will be dug. During the dry season, the lack of toilets is not a problem, but when the rains come, the waste washes into the river, the camp's main source of water for drinking, cooking, and bathing. People know the water is dirty, but it is easier to use it than to carry water from other places. There are not enough pots for making food, much less for boiling and purifying drinking water.

The children take advantage of the river to wash their clothes. There

Washing their clothes in the river requires the boys to work together.

is no soap, so they scrub their clothing on the smooth rocks by the river's edge. One boy dives into the water and soaks the clothing. He passes the wet clothes to the washer, who scrubs them on the rocks and hangs them on bushes to dry.

Staying healthy and clean in Natinga is difficult for the boys, especially without mothers and fathers to help them keep their tukels and their bodies clean. The teachers and older boys can instruct them in basic tasks, such as bathing in the stream and brushing their hair, but there is not enough time or enough adults to care properly for so many boys.

Swimming in the cool river is the best way to spend a hot afternoon.

RECREATION

The boys of Natinga have little free time. Usually there is an hour in the afternoon for them to play, but all of their schoolwork, food preparation, and laundry must be done first. Children too young for school have more time to play, but even they are expected to help with the chores.

Swimming in the deep pool by the marble waterfall is a long-awaited pleasure. After a heavy rain, the children wait until the running water slows enough to be safe, then they race down the banks, shedding their clothing and hollering. Many of the boys grew up along the banks of the Nile, and they miss their daily swim.

Aside from swimming, the most popular activity is soccer. The older boys, teachers, and soldiers play every Saturday afternoon at four. The five- and six-year-olds collect ashes from the campfires and draw boundaries on the field. On the side of the field, the older boys practice with balls made from rubber gloves and elastic bandages.

A teacher or soldier acts as the referee. After the teams are chosen, the players put on old T-shirts for team colors. The referee blows his whistle and the game begins. The younger boys cheer from the sidelines.

Few people have sneakers and no one has soccer cleats, so most of the boys play in rubber flip-flops or barefoot. Years of walking through the rugged countryside have formed tough calluses on their feet. After

Soccer.

the game, everyone runs to the waterfall for a dip if there is water in the riverbed.

Anyok is also popular. For this game each boy has a stick with a sharp pointed end like a spear. The boys divide into two teams, with six to eight people on each side. One team rolls a round gourd past the boys on the other team. When the gourd passes, each boy tries to spear it with his stick. If a boy hits the gourd, the rest of the children gather around and try to spear it again. Points are given for spearing the ball as it rolls past or after it stops moving.

Anyok is a traditional game in southern Sudan. Before the war, when the cattle roamed freely and the children lived in their villages, boys worked in the cattle camps. The younger children learned how to play anyok from the older herd tenders. They played in the morning,

Boys playing Anyok try to spear a gourd as it rolls by.

before it was time to move the cattle to the fields, and again in the afternoon, while the cattle stayed in a corral made of bent sticks. In Natinga, the older boys teach the game to the children who were taken from their villages before they were old enough to tend their fathers' cattle.

Years ago, playing anyok taught the boys to use a spear so that they could defend their villages and cattle from raiders. Now there are fewer cattle. The war has made it impossible for them to roam freely through fields littered with land mines. Many of the animals have died from dehydration. Guns have replaced spears as weapons.

In the evenings, the boys gather in circles and tell the stories their families told them when they were small. The older boys help the younger boys learn the tales. Because most people cannot read or write, the tribes in southern Sudan have always kept an oral record of their history. Adults passed on each tribe's values and history to the next generation by reciting stories before bedtime or after meals. Now the children tell one another the stories their parents and grandparents once told.

The boys enjoy not only storytelling but singing tribal songs while playing instruments made from oil cans.

Tribal dancing is another way the boys of Natinga spend weekend afternoons. Every Sunday, soldiers from Lorus come to Natinga and dance with the children in a clearing on the outskirts of the camp. The different tribes perform dances from their own regions and cultures.

One of the largest groups of Dinka in Natinga comes from the Bar El Gazal region. When it is time for the dancing to begin, about an hour before the sun sets, the men gather in a large circle. Around their ankles are bells, called gar, made from oil tins and rocks. Many wear headdresses made from shredded food bags. Others have berets or baseball caps with long black tassels and strips of torn cloth tied around the edges. Three boys squat in the middle of the dancing circle, beating on the drums to keep a steady rhythm.

Traditionally, the main goal of the dance is for the men to convince the most beautiful women in the tribe to dance with them. The young

Tribal dancing is one of the ways that traditions are passed along to children who are growing up without their families and tribes.

39

men were taught by their fathers that they can impress women with deep, hypnotic chanting and steady, rhythmic dancing. The dances consist of short jumps and hops. The men stomp the ground with their feet, sending clouds of dust into the air as they mimic the movements of a bull, the source of wealth for the Dinka. They sing about warriors, women, cattle, courtship, and marriage.

The boys gather in a tight circle around the dancers. For many of them, the dances they watch are different from the ones they would have seen at home, but they do not know this.

Boys or adults from about thirty-six of the approximately forty-seven tribes from the South live in Natinga. Each has its own culture and rituals. Once a month, the teachers encourage the boys from different tribes to dance for one another. This helps teach the children about the tribes different from their own.

Father Kinga George feels that tribalism, or rivalry between the tribes, may one day be the downfall of Africa. "Tribalism weakens us," he says. "In Natinga, until you tell them the difference between their tribes, they will never know. They are each other's agemates, that is all. It is society that teaches that one is bigger and better than the other." Tribal wars are still a problem in Sudan. The Dinka and the Nuer still fight from time to time, even in the midst of the civil war.

In Natinga the children learn tribal traditions, but they also learn about the world from American schoolbooks. Their teachers hope that when the war is over, the boys will be able to return to their homes but also be part of the modern world.

A Dinka boy perches in a tree on a hill overlooking Natinga.

THE FUTURE

Before I left Natinga in September 1994, Stephen Abol, the medical assistant, contracted scarlet fever. He says when he is sick he becomes very depressed.

"I need to leave this place," he says. "There is nothing here for me.

Soldiers sing war songs and wave their guns after the Commander's speech on Revolution Day.

There is no teacher to teach me. I'm in grade six now and I am sixteen years old. We don't need to worry about food here. If there is no food here, we can go into the forest and collect leaves and grass. All I am thinking of is my future, my education. Food is not as important.

"What has made me think about my future is my father and mother. They are both dead now. I have also lost two sisters and three brothers. My mother died with my two sisters, and one of my brothers in a car that ran over a land mine. My older brother was told of the accident in Malakal and went to look for the bodies. When he arrived at the accident scene, the bodies were still on the ground and there were soldiers around them. They killed my brother because they thought he was SPLA.

"My older brother that is still alive is in Equitos. When he heard what happened to my mother, my sisters, and my brothers, he went to join the SPLA. He told me not to join the army but to get an education. He is twenty-five years old and he has no education at all." Stephen does not want to join the rebels and he does not want to die.

Every year, on the sixteenth of May, the camp observes Revolution Day to honor May 16, 1983, the day the South rebelled against the North and the war began. The soldiers and schoolchildren parade proudly through Lorus. Soldiers and young men perform their tribal dances. Military leaders address the crowd. "We must fight relentlessly to win the war for freedom, justice, and equality so we may enjoy the march of mankind around the world. There is no shortcut to freedom," says commander David Majok. The boys sitting in the hot sun listen intently.

Before the war ends, some of the boys will join the rebel move-

ment when they are seventeen or even younger. Some will stay with their teachers in Natinga. Some will walk to Kenya to go to better schools in the Kakuma refugee camp. Others will keep moving from camp to camp in southern Sudan, looking for safety and a better life. Some of them will die from violence, from disease, or from starvation. They want peace; they also want to win the war and be able to govern themselves.

Father Kinga George worries about what will happen to the boys when the war is over and they return to their homes. Many of them will feel lost. Those from the rainy areas will see mango trees for the first time. The Dinka from Bar El Gazal will see great herds of cattle for the first time. It will be hard for the boys to feel at home in their native areas after living in exile for so many years.

On Revolution Day, as the sun sets over the mountains, Beda Machar walks up the road to his tukel. He says, "The children here do not know where they were born. They do not know where their fathers' homes are. And it is all because of war."

AFTERWORD

Three years have passed since my time in Natinga, and from what I am told, nothing has really changed for the people living there.

War is still raging in southern Sudan, with the SPLA gaining lost ground from the Khartoum forces. Peace talks have been scheduled for the end of October 1997, and sources say that the fighting is increasing, because each side wants to go to the bargaining table with more momentum than the other.

There are fewer unaccompanied minors in the camp—973 children, according to the last Norwegian People's Aid count, in August 1997. Peter Dut, an NPA relief worker, says that many of the children left for the refugee camp in Kakuma, in northern Kenya, because there are better-equipped schools and more consistent food and clothing distributions than in Natinga.

Also, the movement of people within southern Sudan has slowed in the past few years. But with the oncoming drought and the anticipated escalation of fighting, relief workers fear that more displaced people will be showing up in camps throughout the region, looking for food and shelter. This could raise the number of unaccompanied minors, as well as adults and whole families, in Natinga over the next year.

UNICEF recently began reuniting boys in other camps with their families and arranged for 168 children to return to their families.

NPA has set up scholarships in northern Kenya for 51 of the children from Natinga. Peter says that the unaccompanied minors in the camp are "pushing on with meager resources." They are still lacking in basic needs such as suitable food for children, clothing and shoes, and appropriate learning materials for all grades.

Unless the two sides, the SPLA and the Khartoum government, find a way to settle this conflict, children with or without their parents in southern Sudan will never receive the necessities of life that young people all over the world deserve.

I wish that some of the children could travel to the peace talks and let the adults see and hear how their war has devastated so many young lives. Maybe then the two sides would find some common ground in saving the lives of the innocent children.

October 1997